INDIANA JONES™

AND THE GOLDEN FLEECE

PART TWO

SCRIPT
Pat McGreal & Dave Rawson

PENCILS
Ken Hooper

INKS & FINISHES
Eric Shanower

COLORS
John A. Wilcox

LETTERS
Clem Robins

COVER ART
Russell Walks

DARK HORSE COMICS

Spotlight

VISIT US AT
www.abdopublishing.com

Library of Congress Cataloging-in-Publication Data

McGreal, Pat.
  Indiana Jones and the Golden Fleece / Pat McGreal & Dave Rawson, writing ; Ken Hooper, pencils ; Stan Woch, inks & finishes ; John A. Wilcox, colors ; Clem Robins, letters ; Russell Walks, cover art ; Teena Gores, book designer ; Bob Schreck, editor. -- Reinforced library bound ed.
     p. cm. -- (Indiana Jones)
  "Dark Horse."
  ISBN 978-1-59961-576-9 (vol. 2)
  1. Graphic novels. [1. Graphic novels.] I. Rawson, David, 1963- II. Hooper, Ken, ill. III. Title.
  PZ7.7.M44In 2008
  [Fic]--dc22
                                                                        2008009791

All Spotlight books have reinforced library bindings and are manufactured in the United States of America.

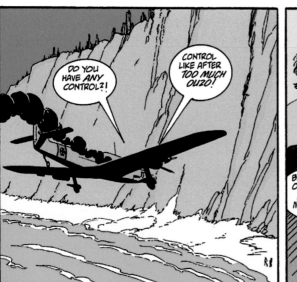

DO YOU HAVE *ANY* CONTROL?!

CONTROL LIKE AFTER *TOO MUCH* OUZO!

BUT YOU KNOW, OUZO IS LIKE MOTHER'S MILK TO ME!

JUST DON'T HIT THE CLIFFS!

OR THE ROCKS!... OR THE WATER!

YOU SHUT DOWN OR I MAKE *YOU* FLY, INDY!

INDY! *HAH!* INDY IS *STUPID* NAME!

FFSSS!

"I SHOULD HAVE KNOWN THEN THAT SOME GREAT HAND WAS AT WORK..."

THAT'S IT! THAT'S IT! OMPHALE, YOU'VE DONE IT! YOU'VE PUT OUT THE FIRE!

OF COURSE! I AM ONE TOUGH CRACKER!

YOU MEAN *TOUGH COOKIE!* YES, OMPHALE, YOU ARE...

YOU BET!

"BUT I DIDN'T CARE *WHY* I WAS STILL ALIVE!"

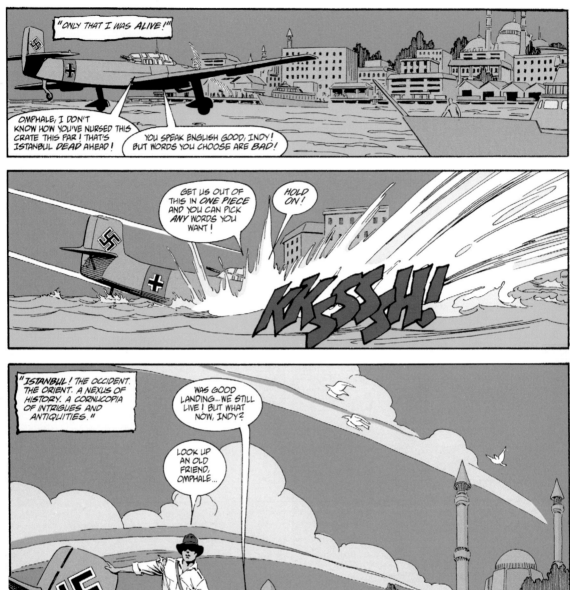

"ONLY THAT I WAS *ALIVE!*"

OMPHALE, I DON'T KNOW HOW YOU'VE NURSED THIS CRATE THIS FAR! THAT'S ISTANBUL *DEAD* AHEAD!

YOU SPEAK ENGLISH GOOD, INDY! BUT WORDS YOU CHOOSE ARE *BAD!*

GET US OUT OF THIS IN *ONE PIECE* AND YOU CAN PICK *ANY WORDS YOU WANT!*

HOLD ON!

KKSSSH!

"ISTANBUL! THE OCCIDENT. THE ORIENT. A NEXUS OF HISTORY. A CORNUCOPIA OF INTRIGUES AND ANTIQUITIES."

WAS GOOD LANDING...WE STILL LIVE! BUT WHAT NOW, INDY?

LOOK UP AN OLD FRIEND, OMPHALE...

BLUB BLUB BLUB BLUB BLUB BLUB

"KNOWING THE DUTCHMAN, DAAN MOST LIKELY HAD A FINGER IN EVERY PIE..."

INDY, DO YOU THINK THIS IS WISE?

MAYBE SOMETHING HERE WILL POINT US IN THE RIGHT DIRECTION.

BUT *BRIBING* AN OFFICIAL IN THE HALL OF RECORDS, FOR GOD'S SAKE! IT'S DANGEROUS! THE CITY IS CRAWLING WITH SPIES AND COUNTERSPIES! IT'S A BOILING POT!

I'M SURE THE GOVERNMENT COULD CARE LESS ABOUT THE TRANSCRIPT OF A TWENTY-YEAR-OLD AUCTION. HOLD THAT LIGHT A LITTLE HIGHER.

THE GOVERNMENT MAY NOT CARE, BUT YOU CAN WAGER *EMNIYET*... THE SECRET POLICE... ARE INTERESTED IN *US*. THE CULT HAS PEOPLE ON THE *INSIDE*. THEY KNOW OF ME.

HOLD ON. WHAT'S THIS?...

LOOK FAMILIAR?

YES. I RECOGNIZE THE DESCRIPTION OF THE PIECES. WE'VE FOUND IT!

WHAT'S IT SAY ABOUT THE FLEECE? IS IT LISTED?

WAIT A MOMENT. I DON'T SEE-- HUH?!

"WHEN WE FINALLY GOT A CHANCE TO STUDY THE AUCTION INVOICE..."

IT'S NOT HERE. NOTHING. NO MENTION OF THE FLEECE. BUT IT'S CLEARLY THERE IN MY PHOTOGRAPH...WHAT CAN IT MEAN, INDY?

BEATS ME...

...BUT MAYBE *THIS* GENTLEMAN HAS A CLUE...

"SECRETARY OF THE AUCTION--MEHMED SARPER." WELL, I'LL BE...

"WE COLLECTED OMPHALE--AT THIS POINT, IT WASN'T SAFE TO LEAVE HER ALONE AT THE APARTMENT--THEN WOUND OUR WAY THROUGH THE MAZE OF MERCHANT HOUSES IN THE BEYOGLU DISTRICT..."

THAT'S HIS SHOP. DEALS A LOT OF OLD JUNK. I'VE BEEN THERE DOZENS OF TIMES AND NEVER HAD THE SLIGHTEST IDEA HE COULD BE OF HELP.

"TURNED OUT THIS MEHMED SARPER, WHO'D RECORDED THE TRANSACTIONS OF AN AUCTION A GENERATION BACK, WAS KNOWN TO DAAN..."

MAYBE. LET'S FIND OUT.

HELLO, MEHMED.

DAAN VAN ROOIJEN, MY COMRADE FROM THE RAINY NORTH! WHERE HAVE YOU BEEN THESE MANY MOONS? I HAVE MISSED OUR TALKS!

I WANT TO TALK NOW, MEHMED. ABOUT SOMETHING THAT HAPPENED TWENTY YEARS AGO.

TWENTY YEARS AGO IS A LONG TIME, MY FRIEND. TWENTY YEARS AGO ALL THIS--THESE ANTIQUITIES--WAS A MERE SIDELINE FOR ME! TWENTY YEARS AGO I WAS GOING TO BE A FAMOUS *PAINTER*! I WOULD SET THE WORLD AFIRE!

AND NOW LOOK AT ME! THE NIGHTS AND DAYS ARE A HASTY PAGEANT THAT FLIES ON WINGS OF QUICK-SILVER. I AM A DUSTY OLD MAN CRUMBLING AMONG HIS DUSTY OLD OBJECTS.
THINK BACK. YOU WERE SECRETARY AT AN AUCTION. TRIVIAL PIECES FROM THE EMPIRE...
THERE WERE SO MANY AUCTIONS IN THOSE DAYS. VEILS OF TIME OBSCURE THE MEMORY.
THIS PARTICULAR AUCTION INCLUDED AN ITEM... A FLEECE... A RAM'S FLEECE. PLEASE. THIS IS IMPORTANT.
DO YOU KNOW WHAT? THIS IS FUNNY! I KNOW EXACTLY OF WHICH YOU SPEAK. I REMEMBER VERY WELL!
WHERE IS IT?! WHAT HAPPENED TO THE FLEECE? WHERE DID IT GO?!
NOWHERE! IT WENT UNSOLD. NO ONE WANTED TO BUY SUCH A MOTH-EATEN OLD THING! I TOOK IT HOME WITH ME! THAT IS WHY I REMEMBER!...
...I USED THE BACKSIDE FOR A CANVAS. FOR A BEAUTIFUL PORTRAIT. THERE IT HANGS!
AND THAT IS THE KIND OF PAINTER ALLAH MADE ME! FOR STILL, AFTER ALL THIS TIME, ALL THESE LONG YEARS, NO ONE WANTS TO BUY!
HUH?

"I STILL DON'T KNOW WHO WAS MORE STUBBORN--OMPHALE OR THE MULES SHE USED!"

I OUGHT TO HAVE MY HEAD EXAMINED!

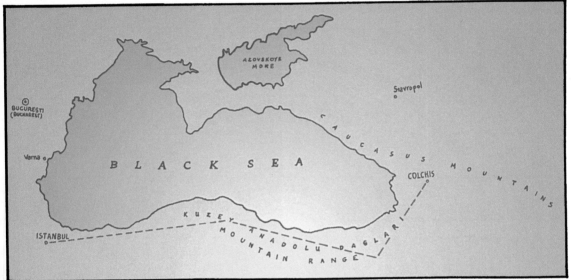

AZOVSKOYE MORE

Stavropol

BUCURESTI (BUCHAREST)

Varna

BLACK SEA

COLCHIS

CAUCASUS MOUNTAINS

ISTANBUL

KUZEY ANADOLU DAGLARI
MOUNTAIN RANGE

"I DO KNOW SHE WAS THE TOUGHER OF THE THREE."

DON'T MOVE AND DON'T LET GO!

HEEAAAAH

"TOUGHER THAN MOST MEN I'VE MET. AND I'VE MET A FEW..."

UP THERE SOMEWHERE...LIES ANCIENT COLCHIS!

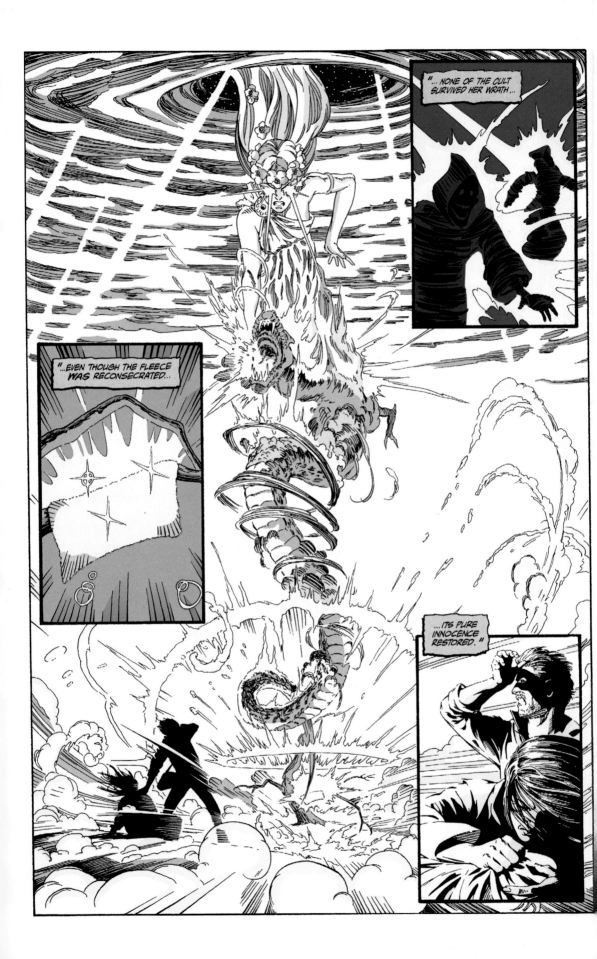

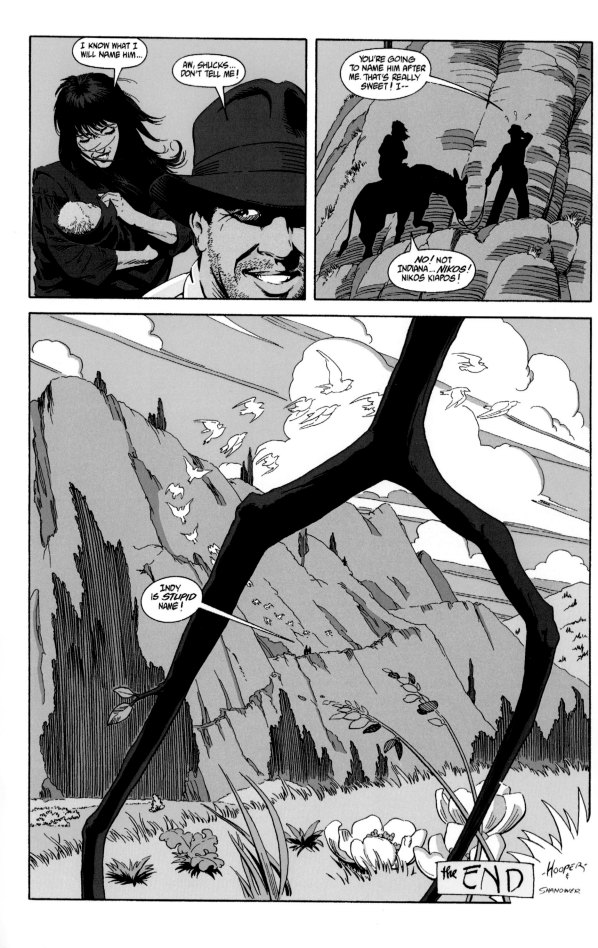